Dear Parent:

Your child's love of reading starts here!

Every child learns to read in a different way and at his or her own speed. Some go back and forth between reading levels and read favorite books again and again. Others read through each level in order. You can help your young reader improve and become more confident by encouraging his or her own interests and abilities. From books your child reads with you to the first books he or she reads alone, there are I Can Read Books for every stage of reading:

SHARED READING
Basic language, word repetition, and whimsical illustrations, ideal for sharing with your emergent reader

BEGINNING READING
Short sentences, familiar words, and simple concepts for children eager to read on their own

READING WITH HELP
Engaging stories, longer sentences, and language play for developing readers

READING ALONE
Complex plots, challenging vocabulary, ar   topics for the independent reader

I Can Read Books have introduced children to   eading since 1957. Featuring award-winning authors a   and a fabulous cast of beloved characters, I Can Rea   e standard for beginning readers.

A lifetime of discovery begins with the magical words "I Can Read!"

Visit www.icanread.com for information
on enriching your child's reading experience.

Spies in Disguise: Lance Saves the World
Spies in Disguise™ & © 2019 Twentieth Century Fox Film Corporation.

ISBN 978-0-06-285298-4

19 20 21 22 23   LSCC   10 9 8 7 6 5 4 3 2 1   ❖   First Edition

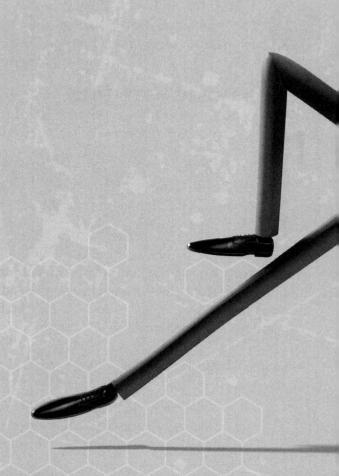

SPIES IN DISGUISE

LANCE SAVES
THE WORLD

Adapted by Tomas Palacios

HARPER
An Imprint of HarperCollinsPublishers

Blue Sky
STUDIOS

Yup, it's me.

Lance Sterling.

Yes, that cool superspy over there.

That's me.

Now get ready.

I'm here to tell you a little story.

This is me on one of my missions.

I'm the world's best spy.

The agency sends me on

the important missions.

I make being a spy look easy.

Look!

I even wear sunglasses at night.

Who knew being a spy

could look this cool!

On this particular mission,

I was looking for some missing tech

that had been stolen.

I discovered these two jokers

in a secret lair.

They have no style.

I should give them

my tailor's phone number.

Anyway, I found the bad guys.

I was hiding inside a fish tank

wearing my high-tech scuba suit.

I decided I needed to

introduce myself . . . in style!

I smashed the glass

and rode over on a giant wave.

Man, I looked so cool doing this!

Of course, I always remember to wear
a clean tuxedo under my scuba suit.
Here I am giving the bad guys
the bad news.

The bad news was that

I was taking back their stolen tech.

Oh, and also they were going to jail.

Yeah, they didn't like

that news very much.

Before I could lock them up,

the bad guys

managed to escape.

But that's no problem.

Because look!

I got the stolen tech back . . .

or so I thought!

I make this spy stuff look easy.

But you know, being a spy

isn't all kittens and glitter.

Sometimes when you're famous,

it can be hard to make friends.

I guess you could say

it's a bit lonely at the top.

Speaking of being at the top,

here's a guy behind the scenes.

This is Walter Beckett.

He's a young lab tech

who builds my gadgets.

So why am I even mentioning him?
Yeah, now we are getting to the crazy
part of this story.

I needed some help.

I know, right?

Me! Needing help?

I was in a high-speed car chase

when I needed to disappear.

Who was chasing me?

My own spy agency!

Why?

Basically, I was framed

for something I didn't do!

So I went over to Walter's house.

He was in the middle of an experiment,

which sort of explains the pink apron.

He said he had a formula

that could make me disappear.

So I drank it.

But I didn't know what the formula did

until it was too late.

Walter birded me.

He turned me into a bird!

Can you believe that?

That's me on the left.

Lovey is Walter's pet.

She likes me a bit too much.

Walter used Lovey's feather

in the formula to turn me

into a bird.

But wouldn't you know it,

as a bird I'm still super fly.

And I still have my brain,

which makes me one smart bird.

I can't drive my car,

but I can fly anywhere I want to go!

Plus, I even met some friends
who showed me the bird ropes.
Lovey was my first bird friend.
Then Jeff and Crazy Eyes
joined the crew.
I should also say that Crazy Eyes
ate one of Walter's gadgets.
Sometimes he burps fire.
Anyway, they helped me realize that
even a superspy can use some help.

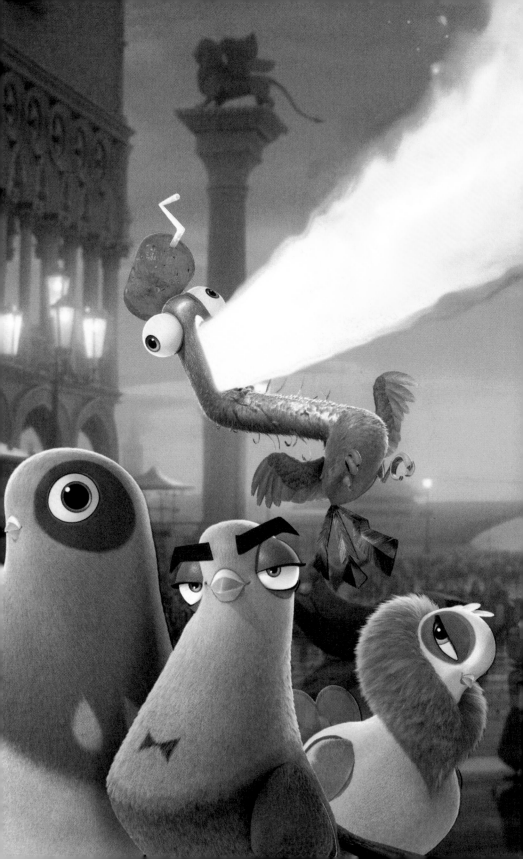

Sometimes I miss the old me.

But I realized something.

I don't need my cool suit.

I don't need my cool car.

Being cool comes from the heart.

Even if your heart

is covered in feathers!

I am happy just being me.

Lance Sterling.

And that is cool!